LOVE
OVER
ADDICTION

With love,
Michelle Lisa Anderson.

LOVE
OVER
ADDICTION

A Guide to Feeling Happiness, Peace and Hope while Loving a Man
who Suffers with Substance Abuse or Drinks Too Much

MICHELLE LISA ANDERSON

Clopet

You are a beautiful woman and you have so many gifts to offer your partner.
You are worthy of love and honesty. You deserve to be cherished regardless of
what anyone tells you or what you tell yourself. Be gentle and kind to yourself
when you read this book. Find a cozy spot, get a cup of coffee or tea and relax–
just for a few moments. I want you to give this book to yourself as a gift. Inside
these pages you will find the tools to transform your day-to-day existence
into the life of your dreams. Imagine yourself waking up and feeling grateful,
excited and full of energy. Take a breath and really imagine it.
You can feel that way, and you don't have to make any major, scary changes in
your life to get started. All the tools you need are right here... at your fingertips.
So, start today and see the transformation occur.

Trust in the process.

You are in my prayers,

Michelle Lisa Anderson.

To Him
And to my love, B

"Be quick to listen, slow to speak and slow to become angry"
James 1:19

Acknowledgements

Did you ever hear someone described as a "good man"? That's my husband: a good man. He is responsible, honest, generous and filled with integrity down to his toes. He's the kind of guy that your parents are relieved that you married. Best of all, he is the perfect example for our sons of who they should become and the type who our daughters should marry. *Brian*, I am so grateful you asked and I said "yes". I love you dearly.

I love my family. I mean, I really, really love them. One of my favorite places on earth is being at home with my six equally wonderful children watching a movie, like Clue. Each one of our kids is unique and will grow up to be amazing, contributing adults. However, to me, they will always be... my little ones. Thank you, *Lance*, *Ellie*, *Lauren*, *Charlie*, *Graham* and *Henry*. You are the best gifts that God has given me.

I have a little brother. But he is not like most little brothers. He remembers birthdays (something I am awful at), shows up for the kid's school events, and plays "creature from below" like no other. He is also one of the most talented and generous musicians out there. He was with me during the difficult years, and he is the perfect choice to write music for this program because he understands, on some level, what we are going through. *Tristan*, I loved doing this project with you. Thank you, butt cheese.

How is it possible that someone can't remember his phone number, but can be one of the wisest men around? My *Dad* is a mentor to many. He is probably the most determined, affectionate and thoughtful man that I know. He has had great success in life. If you need a good story or perfect advice given in a sincere and genuinely kind delivery, you can find him in the French café around the corner from his NYC apartment — just don't ask him for his number. Dad, the older I get, the more I value our relationship — I love you.

A long time ago, I had a best friend who I loved being around so much I thought it would be great if we could be sisters. One year later, our parents got married. *Gary* loves my mom like no other. And my *Mom* is deserving of every bit of love. They are great role models for love. Mom and Gary, we love when your adventures from RVing bring you back home so we can have fun and laughter together.

When I was looking for a graphic designer, my search consumed many mornings and nights. After months, I came upon the website: meganmclachlan.com. Have you ever had the feeling that you "just know" when something is the right choice? That's how I felt when I found *Megan*. I hired her before talking to her. I knew — she was the one to help create Michelle Lisa Anderson and all that involves. Since that moment, I have never regretted my choice. Not once. Thank you, Megan.

Intuition is something I am learning to listen to, as I get older and wiser. When I found *Marisa*, my intuition told me loud and clear that she was the one who would help take my unschooled ideas of writing and make sense of them all. She is another person who I can say is "good". She has been working on this project for much longer than I commissioned her for — that kind of person is a rare gem. You can find her at writingandprstudio.com. (Just don't mention the "working for free" part!)

I'm the type of person who would rather have a handful of really genuine friendships than dozens of acquaintances. I have also been known to be very picky about who is included in "*my circle*". For those of you — I am truly grateful to call you my friends. I will always be there for you. I always will be.

Some might find it strange, but when I started writing this book, I always knew that I wanted to thank the man who inspired it. Although I needed to leave, I am so grateful for the years we spent together. You gave me three beautiful precious peas and many moments of laughter and genuine tenderness. You are deserving of rest and love.

My relationship with *God* hasn't always been easy or natural. I struggled many years to find comfort in something greater than myself. Today, after years of searching, I can say that my joy, peace and happiness can always be found through Him. Thank you for never giving up on me and giving me the gift of loving someone with addiction. I can see clearly now.

Before You Begin

Before we get started, I want you to take a moment to do a gut check. Take inventory of your life as it is today — not as you would like it to be one day or how you think it should be. Take an honest assessment of your life and your feelings about it. Don't worry about the opinions of others for a moment. You don't need to share your answers with anyone for now. And as much as you want to skip this part, don't. It's important.

Are you exhausted?

Are you tired in the middle of the day?

Do you feel lost or empty?

Do you feel envious of other people's happiness?

Are you resentful of your loved ones drinking or drug habits and the hurtful choices they are making?

Are you full of anger, rage and blame about your relationship?

Do you walk around wishing you could be in love with someone else?

How are your relationships with others?

Is there conflict?

Do you feel helpless?

Are you losing friends or distancing yourself from people you enjoy being around?

Are you turning down invitations with others so that you can monitor his bad habits?

Do you have children?

Are they acting out because of the chaos that is going on in your home?

Are they having issues at school with homework?

Do you feel exhausted as a parent?

Are you too worried about him to be present and in the moment with your kids?

Are you angry at him for not being the father he should be?

Are you scared to start planning a family with him due to his poor choices?

I am not asking you these questions out of judgment. I am asking you out of experience. I too have felt many of these emotions, and it's normal and natural to feel this way.
Try not to judge yourself; instead congratulate yourself for being honest.

Now keep reading this book, because the answers to help you are next...

01

Will He Ever Become the Man I Know He Can Be?

Is your loved one everything you want him to be and more when sober? Does he fulfill your needs or desires when he is healthy? Does he give you the love and attention you need when he has temporarily quit drinking or using drugs? Or what if I asked you: do you feel that if he just had the right job and made the right amount of money that everything would be fine? If the outside circumstances changed, would he finally be able to get sober for good?

There is no doubt that your loved one has amazing potential, as we all do. Perhaps this person has found career success or is an excellent parent. We all have our own unique gifts ranging from great communication and social skills to excelling in academics or the arts.

The truth is that people who have issues with drugs and alcohol are quite often some of the most gifted and talented people we know. However, this potential can be masked and covered up by too much drinking or drug use.

You have needs, desires and dreams for your loved one. But it is important to be honest and accept what this person is capable of offering you now. It is critical for your growth to see this individual for who he is today, and not the potential of who he could become tomorrow.

Hanging on to a false sense of hope is going to bring you constant disappointment and, yes, pain.

Tool: In your journal write down all of the positive traits that your partner offers. Then write down the negative traits. Be honest. This exercise will help you to understand what he can and cannot offer you today.

Accepting your life as it is today will help you to begin healing tomorrow.

02

---

*Does My Partner Really Have
a Problem, or is it Just Me?*

Does your loved one have an addictive issue? If you purchased this book, more than likely, the odds are good that you are not imagining that there is an problem.

I have read many, many books and periodicals on the subject of substance abuse over the years. I have spoken with some of the top specialists at elite rehab facilities that witness and care for alcoholics and people who abuse drugs every day. What I have discovered is that substance abuse is not selective.

All too often we believe that substance abuse is only a real problem if you are homeless, uneducated, dirty or poor. However, this is simply not the case.

Alcoholism isn't necessarily the guy in the movies who wakes up and needs a fifth of vodka to face the day. Struggles with addiction can impact a soccer mom, lawyer, doctor, movie star or mailman. From all outward appearances, these people look like everyone else.

Tool: Observe your partner the next times he drinks or abuses drugs. Then ask yourself:

Did he exhibit embarrassing behavior?
Did his friends drink too much or use drugs?
Has he ever missed work or family responsibilities because of his drinking or drug use?
Does he hide his alcohol or drugs from others?
Has he tried to quit and been unsuccessful?
Does he drink or use drugs alone?
Does he escape with drugs or alcohol to avoid stress and depression?
Does he have a DUI?

If you answered yes to some of these questions — this guidebook can help. You don't need to wait for a professional diagnosis to begin your healing.

Nº

03

Can I Help Control His Drinking
or Drug Use?

In the beginning of this book, I stated that I would be honest with you. The truth is there are no shades of grey on this answer; it is simply and undeniably, "no."

A key part of the process towards creating the life you want is being honest with yourself. If you were truly honest, you would admit that all you have done, or not done, hasn't worked. Why? You have no control over someone's addiction.

As you may have learned, there is no amount of willpower that you can provide to another person. There is also no threat, motivation, or consequence that will be effective. Any seeming victory is always temporary or fleeting.

But don't stop reading; there is good news!

You can still feel happiness, a deep sense of peace and an abundance of love in your life, even if your loved one is still drinking or using drugs.

How is this possible?

You do have a great amount of control over someone... You! It really is that simple. You can't control the actions of your loved one that is abusing drugs and alcohol; it's impossible. But, you can learn to control yourself, your actions and your reactions to others. Controlling your behavior is critical to your happiness.

Tool: The next time that you start to feel anxious, angry, or panic because of loss of control, ask yourself: What can I do for myself right now — in this very moment — that would make me happy? Now, go do it! And watch how powerful you will begin to feel.

You deserve a peaceful life.

*Did I Do Something That Caused Him
to Drink or Use Drugs?*

Your love for the people that you cherish in your life may lead you to blame yourself. This is natural. In fact, this tendency is born out of hope. You are hoping to find a way to change your actions and, as a result, change his.

Never lose sight of the fact that you didn't hold the bottle to his mouth or tell him that he should do a line of cocaine. You didn't stick him with the needle or force him to swallow the pill. You must understand that he made this choice for himself. Only he is responsible for his decisions. In every case. Always.

The only behavior you are responsible for is your own behavior. If you choose to nag him, shame him, or yell at him about his drinking or drug use, that is your choice. You need to be held accountable for your behavior.

Can you help your loved one by reminding him of his inappropriate behavior? No. The truth is it is a waste of time and energy to lecture him the morning after a drunken episode. Your scolding will not teach him a lesson or get him to change his patterns of behavior.

Again, you can only control yourself. Just as you cannot control the weather, you cannot control whether a loved one chooses to use drugs or abuse alcohol... not today, not tomorrow and not next month. The only thing that you can control is your responses to the choices that this person makes. Your loved one's behavior may make you feel powerless, but you are not. You have the ability to control how you react to any situation you are in.

Tool: When you see him making bad choices, keep your mouth closed. Walk away. Get busy with your business, and stay out of his. I know this is incredibly difficult, but it's your ticket to feeling better, so keep trying!

*Can I Ever Feel in Control
of My Life Again?*

You can take control of your life right now, today, in this moment. Notice the key word is — "your."

I understand that life can feel very out of control and lonely when you love someone who has a problem with drinking and drugs. I understand the devastating impact this situation can have, as well as the depression, loneliness, anxiety and anger that can overtake you.

It is important that you remember it feels this way because you are giving away your power. You have given him the power to manipulate the pendulum of your feelings back and forth as he pleases. If he is happy and sober, well, it's a good day and you are happy as well. If he is sad and depressed, then you feel anxious, worried and generally miserable. This is no way for you to be! You deserve better.

If you choose to live this way, then your feelings are completely dependent on another person's behavior. Remember, you are in charge of your own feelings and choices. So starting now, in this very moment, begin taking control of your actions and the way you feel. If you want to have a good day, then go and do something (anything!) that makes you feel happy and whole. Try it!

Tool: Wake up every morning and before you walk out the door, think of all your goals for the day. What do you want to accomplish? Focusing and accomplishing your goals will give you a huge sense of control and confidence. And who doesn't need more confidence?

Take control over your decisions today, and you will begin to feel better instantly.

Nº **06**

---

*If He Got Sober, My Life Would Get
So Much Better, Wouldn't It?*

You are a kind and good-hearted person or you wouldn't be reading this book. If your loved one has success with long-term sobriety, would you be happier? Yes, but not as happy as you think. (And yes, you just read that correctly.)

Caring for someone who has been fighting a battle with drinking or drug use is a difficult process. It has likely taken a great deal out of you. You might be feeling mentally, emotionally and even physically drained. We often take care of everyone else first and put our needs last. We are nurturers, caretakers, and sometimes that leaves us feeling very empty — with nothing left to give ourselves. If your loved one gets sober — it's because he has done a tremendous amount of personal growth and recovery. Now you need to do your own recovery.

You likely have scars, perhaps deep ones, all of your own. These scars are independent of your loved one's battle with addiction. You came into this relationship with a past and there might be some unresolved issues in your life.

Here is a point that is vitally important for you to remember. If your loved one gets sober and you don't successfully heal your own scars, you could send him into relapse! Use this information as a source of encouragement to get started with your own healing whether he gets sober or not. It is essential that you shift the focus from him towards you.

When I took self-inventory of why I was continuing to tolerate his behavior in my life, I identified my payoffs:
1. I was scared to upset anyone and say no. I wanted to please everyone.
2. His sickness made me feel important and needed. I felt good when he called me and needed help.
3. Most of the time I could always compare myself to him and feel superior.
4. Lastly, it was very convenient to be in love with someone with a disease so the blame and focus was always on them — and never on my issues.

Tool: Write down a list of painful memories and ask yourself: Do I have closure or am I still in pain? What lessons do I need to learn from those situations? Use your memories as opportunities for growth.

*How Do I Stop Worrying About Him
All The Time?*

When someone you love is in trouble it is only natural to think about that person a great deal. These exhausting thoughts often consumed a significant part of my day. If you are a woman who has become obsessed with your loved one's drug or alcohol use, then welcome to the club! This disease impacts the life of the victim and everyone who loves them too.

Your obsessive thoughts about him are due to your strong desire to control the situation. However, it is essential that you do not, under any circumstances, allow this person to control your actions or thoughts. This isn't the path towards a happy and fulfilling life for you.

You must let it go!

It is time to control your own thoughts. Every time you "go there" and start thinking about your loved one's addiction, you need to take action.

How can you break the control this disease has over you and your emotions?

Tool: The first step is to become aware that you are giving this situation your mental energy. You should then begin to redirect your thinking by imagining or doing something that gives you joy. Think of a happy memory, play your favorite song and sing along, or enjoy an inspirational book or movie. It is time to retrain yourself.

You are not powerless. You are powerful!

You are not a victim. You are a survivor.

You can begin to live a happy, empowering life — beginning right now.

08

Will He Ever Change?

So many of us women who get into a relationship think, "If he loves me enough, he will change." Or, we believe something along the lines of: "I know that once we get married, or once we have children, then he will become the man I know he can be."

Your loved one must want to change... and want it desperately! After all, if he wanted to change badly enough, he would. Think of it this way, if he has a car, he can drive to an AA meeting. If he has lost his license or doesn't have a car, then he can call a friend, or ask you to drive. He can use a computer or a cell phone to get the information necessary to find help. If he truly wants to find help, there are countless ways that it can be found.

Here is the harsh truth; your loved one isn't getting better because he doesn't want to get better.

Accept your loved one for who he is today. Then you can begin healing and to start living the life that you deserve.

Tool: Do not research support meetings, purchase books or throw away his drugs and alcohol any longer. Stop providing tools to help him get better. Give yourself permission to take a rest from the therapist role. He will get help when he is ready. The more you encourage his healing, the more he will resist it.

09

How Can I Start To Feel Better Today?

Let's start by asking another simple question, "How have you been neglecting yourself?" What pleasures and joys in life have you been denying yourself because you are too concerned with your loved one's addiction?

Have you been staying at home and turning down invitations with friends because you don't want to leave him? Do you refuse to spend money on your clothes, haircuts or hobbies because you feel guilty? Has your career suffered because you are too busy taking care of everyone else?

You've been placing your loved one's needs first, and that behavior simply must stop today! You are not a martyr. You are a strong and courageous woman. If you don't feel that way yet (and odds are you don't) then start making the right choices. You need to make the kind of choices that will allow you to begin feeling like the powerful woman you are.

Tool: Make a list of things (small or large) that you can do in each of these categories: emotional, physical and spiritual. Then choose one thing and put it into practice. Give it power by taking action.

Putting your needs first is the key. Once you begin to do so, your resentment will melt away. Taking this step is empowering.

Nº

10

Should I Attend Recovery Groups?

You also need to recover. Many women who suffer along with a loved one with substance abuse issues miss this fact. Your loved one may or may not find help, but this should not impact your decision to find help of your own. Seeking out people who are going through similar experiences and situations is one of the most powerful and life-changing experiences you can have. You owe it to yourself to experience this kind of healing.

Please remember that there are wonderful people out there who will welcome you with both open arms and a warm smile. They will listen when you talk and support you when you need a shoulder to lean on.

If joining a group seems a little scary to you, I strongly urge you to push ahead and find the courage. This is a vital part of the healing process. Keep in mind that some groups even offer free childcare.

The key is to begin the process. Embrace it with an open mind. If the first meeting you attend doesn't feel right to you, then simply attend a different one. In fact, it is quite common for many women to try out two or three different groups before they feel as though they have found the right one.

By making your attendance at a meeting a weekly habit, you can reaffirm that you are important and that the life that you want to live is within reach.

Tool: Get on the Internet today and research local groups that you can attend. I recommend Celebrate Recovery, a Christ centered group, or Alanon, a non-denominational group, which is a division of Alcoholics Anonymous. Print out a list of meetings and store it in your purse. When you feel moved, attend a meeting.
Keep an open mind and give it a try.

Can I Ever Feel Happy?

Right now, you might be wondering if happiness will ever be an emotion that you can feel on a regular basis. The truth is that many people spend their lives feeling badly about, feeling badly. The expectation that we should feel happy most, if not all, of the time leads many of us to feel exactly the opposite. There is tremendous pressure in today's society to try to feel happy all of the time.

Do you feel that everyone else looks like they have such a wonderful life? Does it seem that they are having a much better time than you are? The end result is that we are left feeling inadequate, not good enough — even jealous. Clearly, this isn't healthy.

There is a secret to feeling happiness in your life even when you love someone who has a drinking or drug problem. The secret is to be grateful for what you have right now, today. Gratitude can change your life and shift your mood in an instant. Gratitude changes your perspective and serves as a powerful emotion and a transformative lens through which to view the world. The power of gratitude can bring you light through the darkest days.

Be aware and appreciate the many things in your daily life that are provided for you- even the small things. This will do wonders to dramatically alter your perceptions.

In order to FEEL gratitude you must be present in the moment. Isn't that hard when you are constantly filled with anxiety about your loved one's habits? Is your mind is always drifting away from what you are currently doing to what you think he is doing — wondering where he is, when he will come home, how your life will ever get better, and what you are going to do if nothing changes. This is completely natural.

Tool: Stop and slow down in the moment. Take a deep breath and notice your surroundings. Say thank you for your daily gifts. This can include anything from the sunset and an embrace from a child to a terrific parking spot. The more gratitude you carry in your heart, the more things will appear in your life to be grateful for. It's just that simple.

12

How Can I Ever Trust Him?

It's so very difficult to trust when you love someone who drinks too much or uses drugs. Let's be honest; he hasn't been honest with you.

You may have even had his lies thrown in your face. Perhaps you have found a bottle of liquor stashed somewhere in your home after he swore very convincingly that he had quit for good. Or maybe he called you crazy for not believing him when he tells you he's sober and then failed a drug test.

More than likely (and for good reason), you constantly doubt everything your loved one says to you. Are you driving yourself crazy with all the fear and nonstop questioning? I want you to know that this is perfectly normal in this situation, and that you are not alone.

You may never be able to trust him again. This is a sad fact and likely difficult to read. But it is nonetheless the truth. So how do you stop constantly feeling disappointed every time he lies to you? Just remember — his destructive behavior is his business, not yours. If you have healthy boundaries in place, it will no longer matter whether or not he is telling you the truth. Instead, you will be focused on your choices concerning your own life. You will stop asking him questions that provide opportunities for him to lie to you that result in painful feelings.

Tool: Before you question him about anything such as, if he remembered to take out the trash or who he hung out with after work, consider your own motivation. If the answer isn't something you MUST know — don't ask. If he made a bad choice, you are not his mother. It's not your job to give him a consequence. If you have successfully followed this guideline, reward yourself. Do something kind just for you. Celebrate your victories.

13

*Can I Get Him to Stop Yelling
or Ignoring Me?*

There are some tools in this book that are absolutely essential for your healing process. Determining how to establish your boundaries is one of the most powerful, life changing tools that you can learn. It's time to master this technique and change your approach to your loved one. This will bring you great rewards. You will reclaim your life and your happiness.

Boundaries are those lines in the sand that you establish and don't let people cross, ever. Caretakers, nurturers and people pleasers often erase personal boundaries for the ones they love.

Someone hurts us and we justify it. We make excuses why it's okay for him to behave in a harmful fashion. We somehow make his behavior our fault, which means it's our responsibility to "fix it."

It is essential for our spiritual growth to retrain ourselves.

Determine your boundaries. Ask yourself what you are comfortable with and define your morals. For example, will you tolerate being yelled at? Will you allow someone to exhibit disrespectful behavior towards you? How do you feel about put downs, threats, sarcasm, cheating or infidelity?

If you don't treat others badly, why should you tolerate that kind of behavior directed at you? If you want people to respect you, then first you must respect yourself. There is no other way. It is time to establish firm, clear and concise personal boundaries.

If your gut is telling you that something is wrong, don't talk yourself out of this warning. Listen to your inner voice and stop creating excuses.

Tool: Make a list of your morals or values. What behaviors are you comfortable with and what goes beyond your boundaries? After you have made your list, it will become very clear when he crosses the line. When this happens you should simply state, "I care how you are feeling right now, but I will not tolerate your behavior. When you are ready to speak to me in a respectful, calm manner, I will be eager to listen." Then disengage from the conversation. No yelling, screaming or further explanation is needed. Take a "time out" and give the situation room to breathe. The amount of respect and self-control that you will feel will be powerful.

Nº

14

Can I Ever Feel Good Enough?

Loving yourself is about accepting your entire package. You have grown out of the person that you once were. Certain things will change about you in the future.

Don't worry about who you are supposed to be or who you will become tomorrow. Instead, accept the person you are at this moment, reading this page. Are you perfect? No. Is there room to improve? Of course, there is. This is the case for everyone — even the woman you secretly compare yourself with (yes, that woman) — even she has improvements to make. Don't compare yourself to others. This isn't the road to long-term improvement and contentment.

Are you allowing someone or some instance to make you feel as though you are not good enough? Not worthy? Are you waiting for someone to come into your life and validate you so that you can finally feel good enough?

Tool: Whenever you tell yourself you are just not good enough or not worthy, think of something that you did that makes you feel proud and confident. Was it your work, or the way you made your child feel better? Did you pick out a good outfit today or make a delicious meal?

Give yourself credit for the little things. You need to start replacing the negative messages you are telling yourself with loving, tender thoughts. Be gentle with yourself.

Write down your positive traits. Make a list of the things that make you... you. What do you love about yourself? Are you creative, good with numbers, thoughtful, dedicated, diligent, a good mother or grandmother? You are lovable, you are worthy and you are beautiful. Don't let anyone convince you otherwise.

1.5

Why Should I Ask For Help?

Asking for help is vitally important for two key reasons:

1. Asking for help teaches you to trust again.

There is no way around it; you've been let down... a lot. People have made promises that they didn't keep. You've been lied to so many times and in so many ways that your faith might be shaken. But it is vital that you give someone a chance to prove to you that everyone is not the same. You must make a wise choice when you trust again or you will leave yourself open to additional disappointment. Finding such a person may take time, but this is an investment that is essential. You matter enough to find someone to help you.

2. Asking for help acknowledges that you are worthy of help.

You've been through a lot, and your needs are important. For far too long, you've been taking care of everyone else, including people that don't truly want or appreciate your help. Let someone else return the favor. You not only deserve to give, but to receive as well.

Tool: People can't read your mind. Don't just sit there and wait for help and then become resentful when people don't meet your expectations. Find your courage and ask. After all, you are important enough to receive the gift of someone else's time.

Nº **16**

How Do I Stop The Need to
Make People Happy All the Time?

Women quite often tend to be people pleasers, caretakers and nurturers. There are many benefits that come with these titles. Being a caretaker means having the ability to love deeply and connect with other people. We have the need to be needed.

However, there are negatives as well. When you feel responsible for making others happy all the time, your needs suffer. If you are a nurturer, then your needs may come last. Or even worse, your needs may not make it onto the list whatsoever.

This, of course, has serious consequences. In the end, you will be left feeling empty and resentful. You may feel drained of energy, as though your gas tank is running on fumes and you are never are able to make it to the gas station. Who wants to feel like that all the time? The bottom line is that no one is going to drive you to the gas station; you will have to do that yourself.

Today is the day that you need to stop and fill up your own tank, restore your own energy and begin living the life of your dreams. You must make your happiness a priority.

Tool: What can you do today to fill your tank? Choose an activity that will feed your soul and do it — don't wait for someone to give you permission. Paint, read, take a bubble bath, buy a pair of shoes, go for coffee with a girlfriend, or go for a run. You are important enough to make yourself important.

17

How Do I Feel Peaceful Today?

What brings you peace? This is one of my favorite questions to ask. Have you ever made a list of things that bring you joy and happiness? If you have never done this, then give it a try. This is a powerful and helpful exercise. It might feel a little indulgent at first, but stick with it. Be open to the possibility that making this list will help you.

The rule is that you must list at least ten things that you can do where you currently live and within the confines of your current budget. These should be things that you can do today or tomorrow. So that wonderful trip to Hawaii can be on your list, but it should be number eleven (unless, of course, you already live in Hawaii).

Tool: Begin with simple things and develop your list from there.

Some ideas:
A warm cup of tea and a bubble bath, reading a good book, the perfect fitting dress, warm chocolate chip cookies, a great conversation with a friend, sand in between your toes, reading a bedtime story, painting a picture, or decorating your home.

Of course, these are just some suggestions. Your answers could be completely different from the ones I've listed here, but you get the idea.

Now that you have your list of ten, you have a second task. You need to do one of those ten things every day for the next ten days. By the end, you'll be shocked at how much better you feel. This task might seem simple to many people. However, making this list and then following it seems difficult to caregivers who put everyone else's needs first. Do yourself a big favor and indulge!

Nº

18

---

*Should I Throw Away His Drugs
and Alcohol?*

It may come as a real surprise to hear that throwing away your loved one's drugs or alcohol isn't going to help him. After all, it is only human nature to remove something that is harmful so that no one gets hurt. But your loved one has hiding places that you are not likely to think of even with a good amount of time and effort. And even if you do throw away all of his drugs or alcohol, he will simply buy more.

One difficult fact to face is that by trying to control the situation, you are, in fact, enabling him. More importantly, your attempts to manage the situation will have no long-term impact. He must want to stop using drugs or drinking alcohol.

No matter how hard you try, the fact is that you can't spend all of your time overseeing his behavior. It's not your job. Ultimately, someone with a dependency issue will not allow you to monitor their behavior anyway. He has a disease and he will find a way to get what he wants, regardless of what you do and how hard you try. Remember that your job is to focus on your recovery from painful despair, fear and worry, and all the time and money you have endured dealing with this disease.

Tool: When you find one of his secret hiding spots, don't throw anything away — leave it. As an additional challenge (I know this is going to be a hard one) don't mention it to him or use it as an argument point later. You can do this — I know you can!

Nº **19**

Should I Threaten to Leave Him?

Whatever you do, you must refrain from threatening a loved one. Threats, especially when coming from co-dependents, are usually empty and he will likely to know by now that you are simply not going to follow through.

A common threat is that you are going to leave him. However, if you don't have everything lined up to leave him permanently, then chances are you will come back, and he knows this. Let's be honest with each other. If you threaten never to talk to him again, he is not likely to panic. He knows he can probably manipulate you back into the relationship.

When you threaten your loved one, this is just a scare tactic that you are using to try to get results. If you refrain from making threats, you will rebuild your credibility. When you are finished with this program, you will have the strength necessary to say exactly what your intentions are. Most importantly, you will be able to back those intentions up and follow through with them.

Tool: When your words are followed by actions, people learn to take your words seriously. Many people talk the talk but don't walk the walk. Do yourself a favor and don't talk yet. Why? Because you and I both know you are still learning to walk.

Together, we'll get you walking soon enough. Just stick with me and put these tools into practice. In no time, you will possess a new sense of strength and clarity of mind.

Nº **20**

Is it OK to Lie for Him?

No matter how hard it may be, you must stop lying to cover up his drinking or drug use. Yes, there will be consequences, but that is the point. Your loved one will ask you to lie to your neighbors, friends, his boss, perhaps even his family, but you need to stand firm. Compromising your values and your boundaries is a surefire way to kill your joy.

He needs to understand with great clarity that you will no longer cover up his disease for him, because you are no longer willing to accept responsibility for it. He will get angry and feel betrayed, but again, there is no other choice.

The odds are he will tell you that you have betrayed him, but you can't give in. Remember that compromising your values for anyone isn't courageous, its a sign of weakness. Living your life with integrity means telling the truth, no matter what the consequences may be.

Tool: Do not compromise your integrity and values. I cannot say this strongly enough because every time you do, a part of you starts resenting yourself. Make a promise to be courageous and truthful — always.

21

*Can I Remind Him of His Promises
and Responsibilities?*

When people fail to keep their promises, it hurts. You will no doubt be very tempted to remind your loved one of his promises. However, resist that urge. He can remember his promises and responsibilities on his own. Reminding him won't "snap him out of it" but instead, will simply be viewed as nagging. Nagging is exhausting and ineffective. It makes you seem needy and even weak. Besides, he will just tune you out! For example, if he tells you that he is going to be home at a certain time, make a promise to yourself that you will serve dinner on schedule. It's OK to eat dinner without him. You politely told him that dinner would be served at 6pm, so give yourself permission to sit down and enjoy the meal that you just made. Above all else, don't sit, wait, stew and grow resentful.

Instead allow yourself to enjoy the meal, perhaps even a little dessert as well. Read a book that you've wanted to read. Take your supper outside and enjoy the sunset. Make it fun and enjoyable for yourself. The bottom line is to begin focusing on your life. The sooner you being practicing detachment, the better off your life will be.
Do not pick up your loved one's mess, ever. You should not treat him like a child. If you cook a beautiful meal for him and he eats the meal, gets up and leaves the dishes for you to clean up, I want you to leave his dishes on the table. You are not his parent.

If your loved one is going to be late for his job, that is not your concern. If he forgets to pay his parking ticket, let him deal with the consequences. The sooner he understands this fact, the better off everyone involved will be. You can then get on with your life and your own recovery.

Tool: By keeping track of his life for him, you are replacing his mother, and not being his lover. If you want him to learn about the importance of responsibility — stop being responsible for him.

Can I Ever Stop Feeling Angry, Sad, Anxious, Crazy? And Start Feeling Happy, Peaceful, Relaxed and Powerful?

There is a popular word in recovery called detachment. You know that you have successfully detached when his bad habits do not cause you to make harmful, unhealthy choices for yourself. You are no longer emotionally invested in his behavior. You do not feel mad, hurt or disappointed. In fact, you feel nothing about his actions — because you take no ownership of them.

If you want to stay in a relationship with your loved one or eventually find the strength to leave, you simply must get to a state of detachment. This is necessary, because it puts the focus off his actions and onto your behavior, choices, and decisions and, of course, your happiness as well.

With enough focused attention and effort, you will lose the emotional investment you once had in him. This will enable your own recovery and help you take serious steps towards the life you seek. Detachment is an essential part of taking back your power and, in the process, taking back your life.

Once you have successfully detached, you will start to make decisions from a place of confidence, instead of insecurity, worry and doubt. You will get back in touch with your soul. Your values and morals will start to match up with your words and choices. You will start to remember the person you were before this disease entered your life. You will get stronger. This will get easier. Life will get better.

Tool: It's not up to you to change him by letting him know how his behavior has upset you. Instead, progress with your goals and dreams and be proud of how you handled the situation.

Nº **23**

_____

Why Do I Feel So Tired?

_____

If you are dealing with someone who struggles with abusing alcohol or drugs, it is no surprise that you probably feel tired or even exhausted most of the time. The stress created by his addiction will cause you to feel this way. Stress hormones cause serious changes in the body. You might not realize it on a daily basis, but the acute stress that he is placing on you is putting your health at serious risk.

Tool: So what should you do? Start taking care of your body. Eat a healthy balanced diet (most of the time), get out of the house and go for a walk, listen to your favorite music in the living room, go to bed an hour early, wake up an hour later, feed your soul with your passions: paint, decorate, read, relax, and meditate. Do whatever fills your cup.

If you never considered yourself a courageous person, now is the time to discover the strength to say no to all the daily demands for an hour and take time for yourself. Now is the time to claim it! Peace and contentment are within your reach. All you need to do is take a moment for yourself, everyday, one day at a time.

Nº

24

Why Do I Need to Feel Perfect?

Being with someone who suffers from an addiction for a long period of time takes its toll on your mind body and spirit. You have likely spent a great deal of time feeling as though you need to be perfect in order to deal with his issues. You may have become your own worst enemy.

Are you paying more attention to the negative thoughts, than all the wonderful gifts and talents you possess? Perfectionism is exhausting.

Release the need to be perfect and the shame and embarrassment of admitting you don't have it all together. In reality, you are the only one that expects you to have all the answers or even know all the questions.
The grass always looks greener on the other side.

Do not isolate yourself. You do not have to be alone. Trust that people will be there for you and that your true friends (the people that really love you) will not judge. Even if you don't have such people in your life, you can find them if you just reach out.

Tool: Get over your pride. Let someone know just how "not together" you are feeling lately. It will feel so good to be loved and nurtured in a way that has been missing for a long time. It will feel confirming to be accepted for who you are and more importantly, who you are not. You will feel grateful and will be able to move on with your own life and your own recovery. I want this for you because you deserve it.

Nº

25.

How Do I Get What I Want?

More than likely you've been so consumed about his future and his problems that you have forgotten all about your own future. That must stop.

You can do whatever you want with your life. That means that you can go back to school, move to a different city, take a vacation, write a book or volunteer to help at a homeless shelter or pet rescue. You can do anything with your life that you desire.

Tool: You need to begin asking yourself a long list of important questions.
Here are a few that you might want to consider:
Where do you want to live?
How do you want to feel in your relationships with your family?
What do you want to do for a living?
Physically, how do you want to look and feel about your body?

Once you begin thinking about YOU and what you want, the answers will flow freely. Write those questions down and try writing out the answers with pen and paper. This process will do wonders in helping you clarify your thoughts and your short and long term goals.

I'm not asking you to change all of your behaviors instantly. I want you to think about your dreams and begin moving towards them. This should be fun and indulgent. Dream big — even if you don't know exactly how it will manifest, just have fun imagining.

It is very important for you to know that you are not alone. There are many women who understand what you are going through. I am one of those women. My intention for this book is to help you see that you are worthy of so much more that you are receiving today. And now I want you to have the courage to claim the life you dream about. There are so many more questions that you might have, so please email me. You can also go to my website and subscribe to the blog—a lot of questions that didn't make it in the book will be addressed. I wish I were there to hold your hand and encourage you personally. I know that you are in pain and I also know this journey is a gift to help you become the woman you were created to be. You can do it! I know you can.

Michelle Lisa Anderson.

MichelleLisaAnderson.com
MLA@MichelleLisaAnderson.com

M ichelle Lisa Anderson was married to a man who suffered with the disease of addiction. For over ten years, she searched desperately hoping to find answers how to help him. She wanted to do something, anything, that would save her relationship and get him sober. Michelle vowed that if she ever found a way to stop feeling pain and shift to a place of peace and happiness—it would become her purpose to share the tools with other women who are looking for answers. After years of searching, she discovered the truth. As she found the answers, suddenly things shifted focus. Her new reality became one that was full of happiness and joy.

S he is remarried to a wonderful man and has a blended family of six children and two very large dogs. She resides in Florida and is living the life she was created to live with amazing joy and gratitude.

MichelleLisaAnderson.com